Cheers to the wild ones,
the weird ones,
the ones that break the mold.
The ones who make others live more authentically.
The ones who never apologize for being who they are.
The ones who bravely step out of the box.
The ones who blaze the way.
The ones who inspire.
The ones who make magic around them.
The ones who live life so fully,
savor every moment,
and know all we have is now.
Cheers to the lone wolf souls,
the wanderers, the creatives,
the "unique" spirits.
Cheers to the beauty that our world needs to grow.
It is your energy that paves the way for change,
healing, acceptance, understanding, compassion,
unity and love. Cheers to you.
Cheers to the wild ones.

This book is dedicated to my daughter, Bella

Little Miss Mismatched
would put on her clothes
and nothing would match
from her head to her toes!

Stripes on bottom,
polka dots on top,
a red fuzzy hat,
and neon flip-flops.

Every day she got dressed, her mother would say,
"You look fantastic. Have a great day!"

But when Miss Mismatched went out to play,
her friends would all laugh. "You're SO silly!", they'd say.

Little Miss Mismatched didn't blink
an eye, and simply replied,
"That's OK!" with a sigh.

Again, she dressed however she pleased.
Sparkles, plaid, and fringe to her knees!

Somedays she wore yellow with red glitter shoes,
a purple lace hat and her pants made of blue.

Little Miss Mismatched
liked to dress fun.
Sometimes she wore costumes
with her hair in space buns.

Other days it was faux-fur
made of purple and red.
With fuzzy cat ears on top of her head.

With striped rain boots and hot pink stockings,
she wore what she liked and there were no signs of stopping.

One day her friend, Jessi
knocked on her door
and had on an outfit
Miss Mismatched adored!
Jessi had donned her
Grandmother's pink hat,
found her Grandfather's tie
that was printed with cats.
She was wearing her Mom's
fancy gold shades
and had put a blue ribbon
in both of her braids.
"Miss Mismatched" she said,
"I thought I would try…
to do something different
and I think it's alright!
You inspired me to wear something fun.
And I think my outfit is quite the home-run!"

Miss Mismatched and Jessi exchanged a high-five.

Both of them having a sparkle in their eyes.

More and more friends wanted to dress up.

And before you knew it, it was the "Mismatched Club"!

Her Mom gently hugged her
and patted her head,
sat her down on the couch and quietly said,

"When you are yourself
-just totally you-
you inspire others
to be themselves too.
Not everyone is meant
to be just alike,
it's your uniqueness
that shines like a light!
Always be YOU,
even when it is tough,
because you and you alone,
are ALWAYS enough!"